Note to parents, carers and teachers

Read it yourself is a series of modern stories, favourite characters, traditional tales and first reference books written in a simple way for children who are learning to read. The books can be read independently or as part of a guided reading session.

Each book is carefully structured to include many high-frequency words vital for first reading. The sentences on each page are supported closely by pictures to help with understanding, and to offer lively details to talk about.

The books are graded into four levels that progressively introduce wider vocabulary and longer text as a reader's ability and confidence grows.

Ideas for use

- Ask how your child would like to approach reading at this stage. Would he prefer to hear you read the book first, or would he like to read the words to you and see how he gets on?

- Help him to sound out any words he does not know.

- Developing readers can be concentrating so hard on the words that they sometimes don't fully grasp the meaning of what they're reading. Answering the quiz questions at the end of the book will help with understanding.

For more information and advice on Read it yourself and book banding, visit **www.ladybird.com/readityourself**

Book
Band
7

Level 3 is ideal for children who are developing reading confidence and stamina, and who are eager to read longer books with a wider vocabulary.

Special features:

Wider vocabulary, reinforced through repetition

Detailed pictures for added interest and discussion

The head helps
The shape of the hammerhead shark's head helps it catch and hold creatures.

hammerhead shark

This shark can hold creatures down and bite them.

16

17

Longer sentences

Captions and labels clarify information

Eat, eat, eat!
The basking shark eats little creatures called plankton.

Basking sharks do not have big teeth to bite plankton – they just scoop them up.

basking shark

plankton

24

25

Educational Consultant: Geraldine Taylor
Book Banding Consultant: Kate Ruttle
Subject Consultant: Dr Kim Dennis-Bryan

LADYBIRD BOOKS

UK | USA | Canada | Ireland | Australia
India | New Zealand | South Africa

Ladybird Books is part of the Penguin Random House group of companies
whose addresses can be found at global.penguinrandomhouse.com.

ladybird.com

 Penguin
Random House
UK

First published 2015
001

Copyright © Ladybird Books Ltd, 2015

Printed in China

A CIP catalogue record for this book is available from the British Library

ISBN: 978-0-723-29512-9

Sharks

Written by Chris Baker
Illustrated by Daniel Howarth

Contents

Scary sharks?

Some sharks have very big teeth and look scary.

great white shark

A scary shark!

Other sharks are not so scary.

dwarf lantern shark

Some sharks are very little.

Sharks that hunt

Some sharks, like the great white shark, hunt other big sea creatures.

Sharks look for food.

great white shark

Sharks find food

Many sharks can see very well. This helps them find creatures to eat.

The shape of a hammerhead shark's
head helps it to see well.

hammerhead shark

Sharks catch food

When great white sharks see a creature to eat, they can swim very fast to catch it. When they catch food, they bite it.

This shark swims fast!

This shark bites its food with its big teeth.

great white shark

The head helps

The shape of the hammerhead shark's head helps it catch and hold creatures.

hammerhead shark

This shark can hold creatures down and bite them.

17

Shark teeth

Great white sharks have many teeth. When a shark's teeth come out, it will get new ones.

great white shark ⸺

A shark can get thousands of new teeth!

Shark shapes

Many sharks have shapes that help them swim fast in the water.

mako shark

This mako shark can swim fast.

The great white shark's shape
helps it go fast.

great white shark

This shark does not swim fast.

Basking sharks

Basking sharks are very big.
They might look scary, but
they are not.

Basking sharks do not hunt big
sea creatures and they do not bite.

basking shark

Eat, eat, eat!

The basking shark eats little creatures called plankton.

basking shark

Basking sharks do not have big teeth to bite plankton – they just scoop them up.

plankton

Basking sharks' food

Basking sharks are so big that they have to scoop up and eat millions of plankton.

basking shark

Basking sharks eat millions
of very little plankton.

plankton

Little plankton look like this.

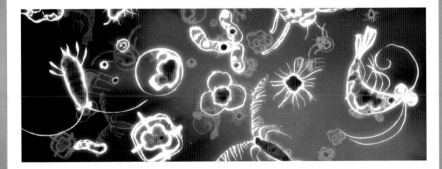

Big and little sharks

Some sharks are big and other sharks are little.

basking shark

The basking shark is VERY big.

The dwarf lantern shark is VERY little.

Glow-in-the-dark shark!

The dwarf lantern shark swims
in the dark sea where it can
glow in the dark.

dwarf lantern shark

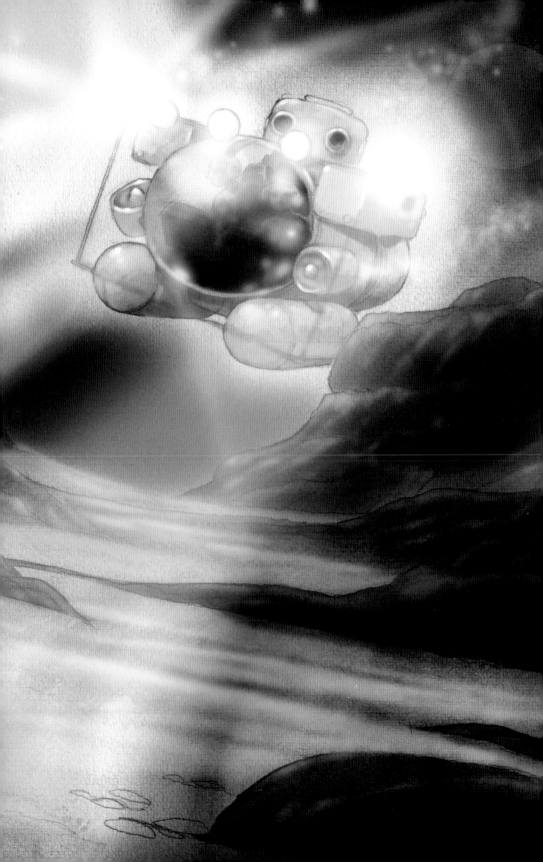

Shark babies

Shark babies are called pups.
Some pups come out of an egg.

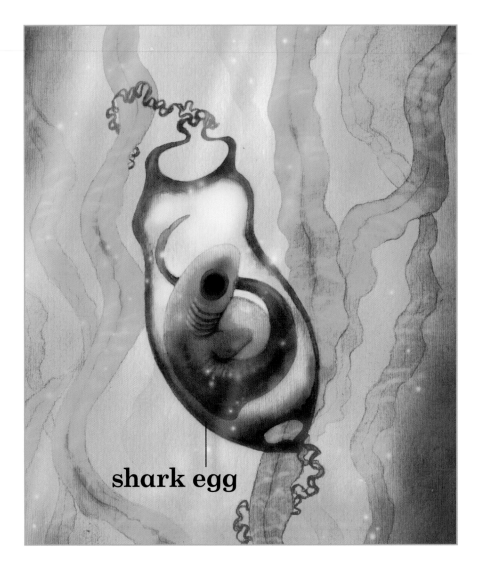

shark egg

This shark pup comes from an egg.

Many shark pups do not come out of an egg. Their mothers give birth to them.

mako shark

shark pup

The mako shark gives birth to pups.

Pups look after themselves

When shark pups are born,
they can look after themselves.
They will swim and hunt.

shark pup

These mako shark pups can
hunt when they are born.

Shark journeys

Some sharks go on great journeys.
One great white shark went from
Africa to Australia and back.

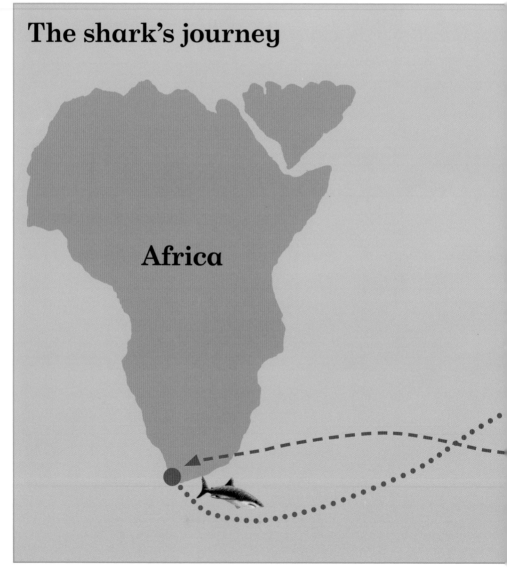

The shark's journey

Africa

The shark went on a journey of nineteen thousand kilometres.

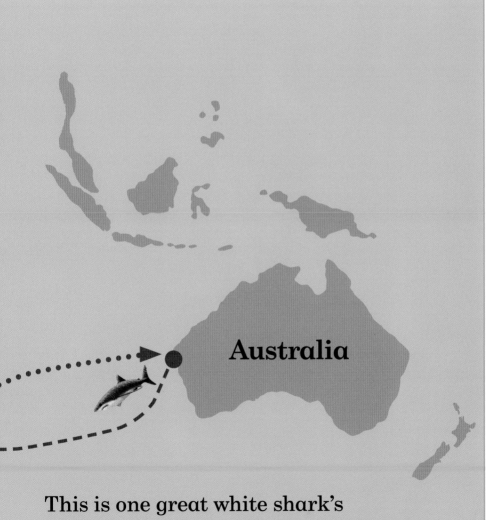

This is one great white shark's nineteen-thousand-kilometre journey.

Swim, swim, swim!

Many sharks must swim all the time. They can't breathe if they don't swim all the time.

These hammerhead sharks must swim
all the time so they can breathe.

Shark attack!

Many sharks attack and eat other sea creatures. But sharks do not often attack or eat people.

Sharks do not often eat people.

Which sharks?

If you went down in the water,
which sharks would you like
to see or swim with?

The scary great white shark.

The big hammerhead shark.

The very big basking shark.

The little dwarf lantern shark.

The fast mako shark.

Picture glossary

 basking shark

 creatures

 dwarf lantern shark

 great white shark

 hammerhead shark

 mako shark

 plankton

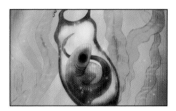 shark egg

 shark pups

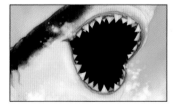 teeth

Index

Sharks quiz

**What have you learnt about sharks?
Answer these questions and find out!**

- Can you name a shark that hunts other big sea creatures?

- Which shark eats lots of plankton?

- Can you name a shark that swims very fast?

- Which shark can glow in the dark?

- How far did one great white shark swim?

Tick the books you've read!

Level 3

Level 4